Full of Growth

Full of Growth

Devotional Book

Reganne Nicole Sheely

Published by Tablo

TABLE OF CONTENTS

INTRODUCTION:

Have you ever been misunderstood by the ones you thought loved you the most? This is where it all began for me. My road wasn't always easy. There were times where I felt hopeless, not good enough, like there was no way anybody could ever love me for me. I felt unseen like the world would be a better place if I were not in it. But, what kept me going was the phrase that I continuously kept telling myself, the only thing that I knew to be true about my life and my purpose: the Lord never promised an easy road; He only promised to be my strength and help me through the storms, promising to lead me down a road of growth if I allowed Him to take control.

I pray this book brings people hope that through the storms, you are not alone. The Lord does not create mess-ups. He does not fail or forsake you. There were times when I convinced myself that the Lord was against me. It wasn't until the storms had passed that He revealed the beautiful things He shaped me through them. He was equipping me and making me stronger. And the Lord does the same thing for you. You may feel alone, confused as you'll never measure up or be enough. Like you don't have a purpose in this world and that this world would be better off without you. But, let me tell you something, the Lord isn't finished with you, and I can assure you that He will never give up on you. I can promise you that if you allow the Lord into your heart fully and permit Him to be in control of everything in your life, trusting that He will only prosper you, then your life will change completely. I want to take you along with me on my journey. It wasn't easy for me, but I can say that it was worth it because, during situations that the enemy intended to bring me harm, I found the true love of Jesus.

Growing up in a town where everyone knows everything about everyone is tough, but growing up in a school where you only have about 110 people in your class felt even tougher. All it took was one day for my life to take a turn and for me to realize the true meaning of struggling and what depression felt like. Let me bring you back to my sophomore year of high school, where I was challenged more than I had ever been before. My world, reputation, and self-worth all changed due to one night, one poor decision, one bad judgment call, something that would soon be seen by just about everyone in town, maybe even across different states.

Your experience might be different than mine. But here's what happened to me and where my journey with God began: I allowed someone that was a friend, video me vaping while holding a baby, which happened to be sent to numerous people, who then sent it to more and more people. Right then, I realized that one single mistake that did not define me as a person was about to change my life forever. I attended a small Christian school, so I would suffer consequences for my actions, which I completely understood. But, it wasn't just the three days of in-school suspension that I had as a punishment. The bullying that followed would be much worse from the people who were once considered my best friends and the people who I had been there for when they felt like their lives were falling apart, constantly calling me "baby killer." Classmates constantly looked at me and laughed as I walked down the hallway. Teachers and administration that were supposed to be the Christian examples treated me differently due to what had happened, and some didn't take the proper actions to protect me.

But, it wasn't just the people in my school that participated in making fun of me. People in other schools took hold of my mistakes and plastered them around social media like it was a funny joke, something to make me feel even worse about myself. I lost my faith, and I pushed God out because if the people who were modeled as Christians treated me like that, I didn't want to be a part of it.

One mistake that didn't define who I was caused me to become depressed. I became eager for my parents to finally let me sleep alone, shower alone, or use the restroom alone, because the moment that I did, I had a plan to end it because I believed what people were saying about me. I believed "you're worthless," "You deserve to die," "you're a baby killer." I could go on and on with the spoken comments and the number of tweets and posts posted about me. I allowed people to determine the way I thought about myself when they had no clue what had happened, the relationship that I had with the baby's family, or the ways that I was making things right with everyone that could've been hurt in the situation that I had caused.

Something that I didn't realize in the midst of all of this was how the Lord was bringing me to hope for the future. He did this by sending me people who shaped me into a better person. The Lord surrounded me with parents who were willing to fight for me and be my rock through the unthinkable experiences of life. He gave me three sisters, who were my backbone and greatest defenders throughout this tragic experience. It was the baby's family who poured love, strength and showed me the true meaning of forgiveness; by the way, they wrapped me in their arms after I had hurt them. The coach who went 'to war' with me and texted me every day, reassuring me that I had someone behind me to love and protect me. My freshman year English teacher came to see me during the in-school suspension in tears, with a note and chocolate, lending the support and love like a true Christian. The small handful of teachers came by to tell me that everything was going to be just fine and that they believed in me. My sophomore geography teacher responded to my email apologizing for what I had done by saying, "the only disappointment that I have during this time is not having you in my class and not being able to teach and love on you." The two best friends, plus my two volleyball best friends, did not turn their backs on me like the others but instead revealed what true friendship was by seeing me the way God created me and loving me for it. The Lord sent me a curly-haired lady who changed my life more than I ever thought possible and turned my life around. He did this because He promises to fill us up with everything that we need at the perfect time. These people stayed and gathered around me, even when I had disappointed them and gave them every reason to walk away and turn their back on me. They helped me more than they could imagine, but it didn't erase the pain that I was going through.

One night, I found myself on my knees, crying out to the Lord, asking Him, "Why would you do this to me?", "Why me?""Why do you hate me?" - and right then I realized something - John 16:33 says, "Here on earth you will have many trials and sorrows." God never promised me that I would never be hurt. God didn't promise me that I wouldn't feel heartbreak. There will be tears, but I had to realize that the feelings of betrayal and hopelessness, feelings of not being enough, hatred of myself - all of those things weren't of God. None of those emotions that I felt were of Him because they aren't who He is. Instead, they were what the enemy was trying to make me believe of myself.

The Lord wants what is best for us, but the enemy loves to see us struggle. We decide to keep our eyes turned toward the Lord, trusting His plans - or to fall in the trap of the enemy. We decide to fall within the love and care that the Lord is eager to offer us. Or believe the lies that the enemy is trying to put into our minds to turn us from the Lord because the enemy knows that the Lord wants what is good for us.

I learned from this season in my life of hopelessness, not feeling enough, and suicidal thoughts were that the Lord never gives up on us even when we are at our ugliest. He loves us more during those times. The Lord never shut me out even when I gave Him every reason to and when I did myself, He waited patiently for me to come back to Him so that He could retake control. One thing about the Lord that is so beautiful is that He never gives upon us, but He will never force Himself upon us. What I mean by that is, He will never force us to receive His love and guidance, but He will wait for us to allow Him to have the power of transforming our lives into something more beautiful than we ever imagined possible. He wants to be involved in our lives, and He is eager to transform you into the best version of you possible, but you can't be that without Him.

This is the book of healing. For the ones who are ready to feel alive again. For the ones who are willing to go through the hurt, insecurities, and scary conversations to heal the wounds that the Lord has been waiting to conquer with you. For the ones that have desperately been waiting to feel loved, energetic, and lively again. The Lord has been waiting for this moment with you, as He did for me. Let's conquer this together. Xox.

At the end of each chapter, you will find a fight song, prayer, reflection. These are some things that have helped me through my journey, and I pray that this will help you.

Reflect:

What is one question that you have always wanted to ask the Lord?

Close your eyes and ask Jesus three words that He would use to describe you.

What are three things that you felt have held you captive and that you have wanted to let go of?

What do you need God to clarify to you? What do you need to sacrifice to change those feelings?

Are you willing to put forth the effort of transforming your life into something more beautiful than you could ever imagine?

What are three things that you know to be true about God?

CHAPTER ONE: YOU ARE NOT ALONE

You know the feeling. It is the kind of feeling that comes out of nowhere. The one where you feel like nobody around you notices you. When you feel a constant urge to fake a smile so that someone, anyone, will spend time with you. The enemy finds pleasure in the thought of our suffering. The enemy finds satisfaction in putting thoughts in our minds that are not of God, in the hope of turning us away from Him. But, it is up to you to change that cycle. It is up to you to determine which one you want to follow and which one you want to control your mind.

Do you want a Father who brings peace, laughter, and a future? A father who is madly in love with you. The Lord wants us to seek His love and guidance. The Lord promises never to fail us. There may be situations in your life where you feel like the Lord has punished you, but the Lord keeps His promises. The Lord wants **you** to know that everything that the enemy intends for your harm; the Lord is working on turning that around and making it for your good.

Remember this - the Lord has never abandoned you. Even when you thought that you were alone. During the nights that you were lying in your bed crying, convincing yourself that the Lord didn't care about you or ever hears you - He was actually the one sitting on the edge of your bed, crying WITH you.

He was the one looking at you, wiping your tears, and waiting for your voice to ask Him to rescue you. He wants to rescue you. There is not one thing in this world you could do that would cause Him to turn His back on you because the Lord created every single inch of who you are. The Father of this Universe created you. He hand made you, and He treasures you. He promises never to allow us to go through anything alone. There is nothing that none of us can't conquer when we put Him in charge and allow Him to conquer it with us.

In Psalm 46:1-2, the Lord is talking to you by saying, "God is our refuge and strength, an ever-present help in trouble. Therefore we will not fear, though the earth gives way and the mountains fall into the heart of the sea."

He clearly states in His Word, do not fear because He is willing to be your rock, your shelter, and your strength. He will never leave us out to dry; instead, He is willing to come alongside us and conquer the darkest days with us. He is ready to transform you and prove to you that He will never allow you to be alone ever again because that feeling doesn't come from Him. It comes from the enemy, himself. The Lord will be your shelter, holding you up when you feel like falling to the ground covered in all of your insecurities, struggles, and depression. He has always been the one sitting right there with you, crying with you, and holding you in His arms. He has been aware of your thoughts and struggles, waiting for you to acknowledge that He can conquer this for you if you allow Him to. It's time not to fight this alone, sister. It's time to stop letting the enemy have power over you and give the glory back to the One who is in awe of your every move and is crazy in love with every little thing that makes you who you are.

Chapter "fight" song: "Jesus I Believe" by Big Daddy Weave.

"Lord, I praise You for always being there when I felt alone. Thank You for never being ashamed of me and for loving me past my lowest days. I ask that you would reveal Yourself to me during my time of feeling alone, and I won't even be able to deny that it was You. Thank You for being my best friend, even when I didn't feel it, and for never leaving my side. I need You, Father, and I need the sense of security and protection that only You can give me.

Amen."

Reflect:

Where do you run when you feel alone, and how do you cope with the things going on in your life when you feel the most alone?

What are things that you can do to make sure that you incorporate God throughout your hardest days?

CHAPTER TWO: YOU ARE NOT A MISTAKE

The lies that I allowed to consume me when I made that one bad decision sophomore year. The lie that I was a failure. The lie that people spoke over me that I was better off to end my life because I was such a horrible person. The lie that I told myself that I was a mistake, and this world would be better off without me. All of those lies were not from the Lord that created me. They were lies spoken out from the enemy that was anxiously waiting to destroy me. If you struggle with believing the lies that make you feel like you are constantly looked over and not enough for this world, like you are a mistake - let me reassure you of the things that the Lord wants you to know right at this moment.

When God made you, He worked intentionally and carefully, crafting your personality, looks, goals, and skills, even allowing your imperfections. He spent time on you because He knew the magnificent things you would accomplish throughout your lifetime. Through that, He purposely installed things in you that He knew you would need to conquer the things that life would throw your way. God knows all of the things that make your heart smile, all of the things that you dream to become, but what's even more beautiful? He equipped you with everything that you needed to fulfill the things that you dream of. You were intentionally made.

You are perfectly made. You are His prized possession. What's more? God wanted **you** on this earth to help strengthen His Kingdom.

The Lord spent so much time on you, already knowing your name and your purpose, and He wants you to succeed and fulfill all of the magnificent plans that He has in store for you. God doesn't create mess-ups. He has never once made a single mistake - the moment that you start telling yourself that you shouldn't be here and that you were a mistake - remember that God spent so much time on you, and He doesn't regret a single thing about who you are. You are so special that God sent His only Son to die so that you could wake up every single day and fulfill your purpose.

The Father wants you to pursue your given talents, glorifying, and honoring Him. God knows you. He knows the things that hurt you the most, but also the things that fill your body and heart with excitement. He knows what you fear, but He also knows what makes you eager. He desires to be connected with you and within you. He wants a deep, close relationship with you because you mean that much to Him. You are one of a kind. God made nobody else like you because He knew you were the only one capable of fulfilling what He has in store for you, and I promise that purpose is so beautiful and life-changing. Honor yourself that way. In so doing, you are honoring the One who made you.

Chapter "fight" song: "Pieces" by Bethel Music and Steffany Gretzinger - this is how passionately Jesus loves you.

"Father, I pray that during the times when I feel like I'm not intended for this world and like I am a mistake, I ask that you reveal to me who you are. I ask that you fill me up with reassurance of Your love and remind me whom you created me to become. I praise you for installing me with everything that is of You and for spending time on me. I ask, Father, that you would help conquer my own thoughts, telling me I am a mistake, and replace them with only things that are true of You. Amen"

Reflect:
When do you feel the closest to God?

When do you feel the farthest from God?

Try to recall a time in your life when you felt like a mistake, and try to picture God in that situation.

CHAPTER THREE: GOD IS PREPARING YOU

Say this aloud: God is preparing me.

There have been many times in my life when I convinced myself that I wasn't capable of overcoming the depression that had filled my life. I convinced myself that I would have to live in a world where I constantly felt as though everyone else had their life together, while mine seemed to be falling apart piece by piece, day by day. I allowed myself to believe that I was not in God's plan. I convinced myself that God was no longer preparing me for something great because of the poor decisions that I had made in the past. Have you ever been there before? Let me transform something for you.

Let's start living by God's Word in Romans 8:28, which says, "We know that God causes all things to work together for good to those who love God, to those who are called according to His plan."

The only way for the Lord to actively blend all of the things in your life is when you decide to live according to His purpose instead of your own plans. Let's take a moment and try to think of the lives that aren't willing to follow God's plan for them actively - their lives are in motion of what they desire for themselves. It doesn't mean that the things in their lives aren't going to pause from playing out and blending because of their decision not to follow Christ, but what it does mean is that their plans won't exceed their highest potential. By allowing God to be at the center of their lives and submitting to Him, things start coming together for not only His good but their good as well. Things that were once confusing begin to make sense. You begin to see the ugly parts of life as an opportunity for growth, a part of God's divine plan, instead of another speed bump in your already rocking road.

Throughout life's knocks and wounds, God is preparing you for the perfect destination that you longed deserved and that He created just for you. It is easy to throw in the towel and give up because things can become overwhelmingly painful throughout life's hardest moments. I have been there more times than I can count. But, if you are willing to keep your eyes focused on God's purpose for you and not your pain, then God will turn your storm into a shining light that you longed for.

When you feel at your weakest, God is at His strongest. There is no experience wasted when surrounded by a Father who is constantly working for your benefit. Keep your mindset focused on the thought that God has an end destination for you that is beyond anything you could imagine. You can't get there without Jesus' help. Lean on Him and trust that He will provide for your heart through the darkest valleys. Trust that your God has your back and is in the works of changing the painful things into something beautiful for your good. God is equipping you for something that you never thought you could ever achieve, but with His hands on your life, anything and everything is possible.

Chapter "fight" song: "So Will I" by UPPERROOM (feat. Abbie Simmons).

"Father, take me along your path. Reveal to me your plans and reassure me that you are preparing me for life You had set for me. Please fill me with patience and grace as I walk into this new way of life with you by my side. Thank you for being constant and for never giving up on me, even at my most ugly moments. You are trustworthy. You are powerful. You are capable. Help me see You in every situation that I am in and when I am struggling, overwhelm me with your love and grace. I love you.

Amen."

Reflect:

Are you willing to give the power back to God? If so, what do you need to let go of for you to get there?

CHAPTER FOUR: YOU ARE NOT BEING PUNISHED

During the times in your life when you feel like you don't want to keep fighting - the easiest thing to do is to lay in bed all day and not continue the life that you were given. When all you feel is weak, hopeless, and broken, the Lord wants to remind you again (like I said in the last chapter) that when you are at your weakest, the Lord is at His strongest. He is at His strongest so that He can be the strength that you desperately need to continue.

If you are a follower of Jesus, He is never punishing you. He created you. He took time on you. Our Father only wants us to succeed and flourish. When the enemy tries to convince us that our struggles, the things that are going on around us are permanent. We get blocked off from the reality of things and convince ourselves that we will never heal...but you will. God is awaiting you and is never blocking you out; He is aware of your every move, and He is active. When you feel like the world is falling apart when the boy you liked breaks your heart when home-life is too hard, and you want to lock yourself in your room when you feel a pain deep in your heart. You feel like you're drowning - be reminded that God is preparing our hearts for the impossible and equipping us for the incredible things that He has set out for us. What's more? God shows up with something better. He did it for me. Why wouldn't He do it for you?

I felt weaker every day. I was never happy. I felt like the Lord was against me and didn't want to hear from me. I thought because of what I had done that God had given up on me because I had failed and disappointed Him. But, God takes the smallest thing to show us what we are capable of. He would never punish you. You are His child, and He is protective over you. He takes care of His children. The Word even clarifies for us in Psalms 103:10

"He doesn't deal with us according to our sins or repay us according to our wrongdoings."

Scripture reminds us that the Lord never reacts to emotions. He never repays us or criticizes us because we do wrong. Actually, He knew that we would fail, mess up, and sin--but He created us anyway. He loves us anyway. He pursues us anyway.

Chapter "fight" song: "Washed" by UPPERROOM (feat. Brett Bell) - you are washed from all of your sins, Jesus renews you every single day and forgives you day in and day out.

"Jesus, thank You for loving me anyway. Thank you for pursuing me anyway. You are real. You are active. I pray over myself right now that instead of allowing my own thoughts to convince me through my toughest times that you aren't near and that I am being punished, that I would instantly be reminded of all that you are. You are One that loves without measure and One that forgives me before I even say sorry. Forgive me for my sins and grow me closer to you. Take me down the path that is destined for me, Father. Thank you for sticking by my side and loving me even when I find it hard to love myself.

Amen."

Reflect:

Try and recall a situation that you were in that made you feel like the Lord was punishing you, and when you felt like He was against you.

Afterward, pray and think about what God was really trying to work in your heart and life during those times

CHAPTER FIVE: LET GOD IN - STOP FRIEND-ZONING HIM

The Lord is eager to work with you during your highest of highs and lowest of lows. One of the most precious characteristics of the Father is how much of a gentleman He is. God respects us, He respects our privacy, and He will never force Himself into our lives unless we ask. That does not mean that He ever will stop loving me, you, or anybody else in this world, because He promises always to love us and watch out for us; however, He will not force Himself into a situation without our permission. He always gives us the option to have a relationship with Him. It won't be until you say, "Jesus, I give you permission to take hold of my life, put it in Your hands, because I trust that You will carry me through your extraordinary plans perfectly, peacefully, and strictly for Your desire and my purpose."

As soon as you give your life to Him, everything changes. The moment that I decided I was done being in control, everything changed. I realized I needed Him more than anything, and I knew he would take care of me. I was on my knees, crying out to the Lord in the middle of the night one night, telling the Lord that I gave Him all of my relationships, my plans, my life, my gifts, and my heart. I gave Him permission to do whatever He desired with it because I knew that He would take out the things that didn't better help me. I knew he would bless me with something greater. And let me tell you, He did.

Over the next few months of my life, He removed me from groups of people I knew didn't better me, but I couldn't do it independently. He gave me the strength to realize my worth and to walk away. He led me to people who made me feel more alive and led me closer to Him. He led me down a path that filled me with constant joy and peace, and I felt His presence more than I ever had before. I dedicated my life to Him, and now it is your turn to change your life around for the better because I can promise you that you will not be disappointed because the Lord is the only One who will truly never fail you or let you down.

The Lord deserves to be a part of every decision you make; He doesn't deserve to be friend-zoned by you. The Lord is the One who never judges you. He never doubts you; He looks at you like you're perfection because, in His eyes, you are. He created you in His image. If for that reason alone, you realize your worth, then move into His arms and give your life over to The Lord. The One who adores you and uses the dark moments for His glory. He will take care of you. I promise.

Chapter "fight" song: "Stand in Your Love" by Bethel Music and Josh Baldwin.

"God, I am done friend-zoning you. I pray that I will allow myself to have the confidence to give control to you because ultimately, you know what is best for me and my life. You are the One who created me and made a purpose for my life. I thank you. You have never left my side, and You promise in Your Word that you never will. Thank You for Your promises that You have promised over my life and my journey.

Amen."

Reflect:

Name the relationship(s) in your life that bring you closer to the Lord and how?

What are things or relationships in your life that are bringing you farther from the Lord?

CHAPTER SIX: THE ENEMY DOESN'T DESERVE TO CONTROL YOUR MIND

During the time in my life when I faced extreme depression. The times when I allowed words of people to define who I was. The time of my life when I could no longer depend on people I had once called friends because they had turned their backs on me, I gave the enemy power in my life to control my thoughts and define me because of them. I started living and believing the constant lie: I'm not worthy of living. The constant words in my head told me that I was a mess up and never be forgiven.

Still to this day, I live a life in a constant battle of the enemy's words and thoughts, but I found the strength to recognize it. The enemy's main mission is to turn our backs on God and for us to think that we will never be able to live a life with constant joy and happiness in our hearts. But, let me remind you of something - you decide to transform and redeem that for yourself. The Lord is waiting for you to feel His full embrace.

The enemy likes putting thoughts into our heads to turn us against the One who actually wants what's best for us. The enemy tells us that your mistakes define you, but the One True Father says that you are redeemed from them because He purposely sent His only Son down on this earth to die for you and resurrected three days later so that you would live a life where God forgave your sins. The enemy wants you to believe that you are not worthy of love and happiness, but the Lord tells you that God chose you and you are made by Him to experience the love that He wants to fill you with.

It is so easy to start to believe the things that the enemy has to say about you--trust me, I have been down that road more times than I can count--but please believe me when I say that the moment you decide that you have had enough of the enemy's control - your world will change in ways that you never thought possible. I still have to do daily when I can feel that the enemy has been putting negative thoughts in my head is called them out. The most down to earth moments throughout my journey were ones when I was forced to face the thoughts inside of my head. The thoughts that I wasn't enough and that I would forever live a life of regret and guilt. However, the Lord graciously gave me an alternative when I was faced with those moments. Instead of allowing myself to sulk in the negative thoughts that I believed to be true, I chose to ask the Lord to replace the thoughts leading me deeper into my depression with thoughts that reinforced how He pictured me. It sometimes took me sitting in my bed, telling the enemy that he no longer had authority over my mind. Doing this allowed me to transform the negative thoughts that I had about myself and turn them into positive things that God says about me. I challenge you to do the same. You, my dear, are worth more and loved so much more than what the enemy has to say about you. You are worthy of being rescued, treated like a queen, and with a respect that only the Lord can offer.

Chapter "fight" song: "Abba (Arms of a Father)" by Jonathan David and Melissa Helser.

"Lord, I pray that I will recognize when the enemy is coming at me, and that with Your almighty power, that you will fill me up at that moment with everything that is You. I pray that You will consume all of me and that the enemy will no longer play a part in my mind. I pray that You give me grace and wisdom throughout my life and that You continue to remind me of who I am when I am at my weakest. Thank you for Your grace and all of the time that You spent with me. I am thankful for You.

Amen."

Reflect:

What are the insecurities that you are ready to let go of?

Call those out. Write them down and look into the Bible and see how God changes the things that you feel about yourself into how he truly sees you.

(For example: If you wrote, "I am insecure of my looks," look into the Bible or online about what the Bible says about my personal appearance? There will be verses that the Lord has given to your answers and questions about your insecurities in the Bible already).

CHAPTER SEVEN: THE LORD KNOWS YOUR OUTCOME

October 28th, 2018, was the day that God changed my life forever. I found myself surrounded by a group full of people who believed in me, loved me, and took the time to help transform me into the person that I desperately wanted to become. Beside me stood the woman who poured strength, the woman who sacrificed countless hours and days to sit with me and guide me through the emotions I felt. This woman helped shape me and molded me into someone I always dreamed of being but didn't believe in myself enough to get there. But, with her guidance, her unwavering faith in me, and her daily reminder that the Lord hasn't given up on me, I slowly became the person that I wanted to be.

On October 28, 2018, that woman baptized me as I was surrounded by the people who believed in me. Right before we got into the water together, I was able to look around at several people that took time out of their Sunday to watch me make the most important decision of my life. I remember the moment before I got into the water; I looked over at my parents and sisters and got a flashback. Looking into their eyes filled with joyful tears, I was taken back to the nights that I laid in my mom's arms as she held me, crying with me as she reminded me of my worth. I remembered the time that my dad looked into my eyes and said, "I'm going to be right here, getting you through this." I was reminded of the message my oldest sister, Courteney, texted me of 15 reasons why I was worth living, worth loving, and why she loved me. I remembered when I saw my second older sister, Lynnsey, for the first time after it all happened, and they embrace that she gave me as she held me as I cried. And last but not least, the times that my third older sister, Lexi, became my best friend and broke the rules of in-school-suspension by storming into the room that I sat in during the school day with tears flowing down her face because she wanted to let me know that she loved me and was there for me.

I wrote in my journal that day that I learned God knew my plans. God allowed the most terrible thing to happen to me because He knew the result. God knew that through my experience, I was going to see Him in a completely new way. God knew that I would start chasing after Him, and He knew that He was going to send me people who could stand in the gap for me when I needed extra support. The Lord uses us as His vessel here on earth. He gave me this experience, this testimony to help people go through the same things and feelings that I have felt. I would go through all of the sleepless nights again for Him if it meant that it got me where I am today.

Are you there yet? Would you be willing to do that? I'll be honest if you asked me before I realized what God was doing; I am not sure how I would have answered that question. After seeing with my own eyes the way that God has the power to turn the darkest moments into the light for you, for me, and all of His children, I realized I would go through that fire any day for Him because He led me through the unthinkable and into something that is beyond all I can imagine - so now it's your turn. The Lord knows your plans, even if they seem super messy to you at the moment. In the end, nothing will stop Him from pursuing you and doing what is best for you. The Lord will never fail you, just like He never did for me. Even during the nights and days when I felt forgotten, the days when I would cry myself to sleep or starve myself because I did not want to live anymore, the Lord knew my result. He knew where I would end up, and He knew that I was filled with strength that I never knew I had. It is the same for you - He knows things about you that you don't even know about yourself, and Your Father believes in you more than anybody in this world will ever be able to. Jesus is awaiting your call to accept whatever you need to overcome to get you to your extraordinary outcome. Are you ready?

Chapter "fight" song: "Defender" by UPPERROOM (feat. Abbie Simmons) - this is my life fight song. Jesus led me to this song during my lowest of lows and reminded me that I have a Defender in Him that protects me, loves me and fights for me. Now, allow yourself to believe that you have a Defender in Him too that protects YOU, loves YOU and fights for YOU.

"Jesus, thank You for the promise that I can overcome the impossible. Thank You for the promise that you are leading me closer and closer to my outcome every day. You are never leaving me stranded alone, and there is never a moment when You have given up on me, nor forgotten my end-result. You are continuously intentional and faithful to my calling in my life. Lead me closer and closer every day to the outcome that You intended for my life. Thank you, Jesus.

Amen."

Reflect:

Are you willing to go through the fire with the Lord to get to your magnificent result? What does that look like to you?

What things can you do with the Lord to help you all connect more intensely with one another?

CHAPTER EIGHT: YOU ARE NOT DEFINED BY WHAT PEOPLE SAY ABOUT YOU

Throughout my journey and when my life felt like it was falling into a million pieces around me, I allowed what people thought and said to become my reality. I allowed people's negative words to play such a role in my life to the point that I started believing in them, defining myself as them, and living by them. One of the reasons I actually allowed myself to believe the horrible things that people spoke over me was because before the situation happened to me, I called those girls and guys my good friends, some even my best friends. It was the people I spent my weekends and free-time with, and even people I had never even spoken to in my entire life - I still gave them that power over me.

But, let me challenge you with something - it doesn't matter if the person is your best friend or someone you just met. The negative and harmful words that people speak over you are powerful and hurtful. Their words and behaviors could start becoming things in your life that are toxic and bring you down, which is something that the Lord never intended for your life. The Lord wants you to be surrounded by people who grow you, make you better, and laugh. The people that intentionally say harmful things that bring you down don't deserve to have that role in your life. If you allow those people to have a say in your life and how you view yourself, then it's time to re-evaluate your friendships because you are worthy of friends that make you better and allow you to see the good in yourself. If you continue to live a life with people who bring you down, you start living by what they say to you and begin telling yourself that what they have to say about you is the truth. Listen to me closely; the only person whose opinion of you matters is the Lord.

The Lord is the One that says that there is never a moment in your life when you are not loved and treasured. Your Father in Heaven tells you that there is never a moment when you aren't worthy of His love and plan for you. So, what makes you believe that what you are worth is determined by people who are far from perfect? What makes you believe that the people telling you that you will never be pretty or good enough have any right in ruling your life when you have a God who pursues you day in and day out? The Lord wants to remind us we will not be treated fairly in this life because people have flaws and will hurt us and say things that bring us harm, but the Lord is flawless. He will remain true to us.

When someone mistreats you, try to view it as a way to grow in grace. That was one of the hardest things for me. I wanted so desperately to seek revenge on the people that intentionally did things that would harm me - but who was I to judge someone else when I am just as sinful as them. I started to view these moments as opportunities for me to expend the Lord's love over them and allowed the Lord to take care of them. Instead of focusing so much on what people have done to hurt you and how they view you, challenge yourself to focus more on the One whose view ultimately matters.

When someone mistreats you, remember that His ways are much better than fair. His ways are peace and love, which have been poured into our hearts by His Spirit. It wasn't until I took a look around me that I realized how much time I spent allowing people who were just as imperfect as me to determine my worth. I have a Father who is the only perfect Being, and he says I am valued, seen, and worth being loved and fought for.

Chapter "fight" song: "Who You Say I Am" by Hillsong Worship.

"Lord, allow me only to hear Your voice. Thank you for creating me with purpose, for taking Your time on me. Thank You for loving me past my mistakes, and thank You for walking alongside me when I forget who I am. Let me down a path where You are in the center. Set a fire in my soul that is passionately for You and only You. Allow my life to reflect on Your purpose for me. I love you, Jesus.

Amen"

Reflect:

What are the things that you have allowed to define you? (take that and look up verses in the Bible that prove to you that the Lord thinks so differently about you. He provided evidence in the Bible for you in His Word; I gave an example of how to do that in Chapter Six)

After you find those things that God truly has to say about
you - write them on a sticky note and put those words in places
that you will see daily to remind you of how God says that you
truly are.

CHAPTER NINE: EVERY PERSON HAS THIER OWN BATTLE

The Lord has laid on my heart that every one of His children is put onto this earth to walk through a different purpose, full of different highs and lows, to be shaped into who He ultimately destined us to become. Throughout my struggles, I compared my life to other people's. I was constantly wondering why one mistake would define who I was and why it felt as if my situation was always the center of the conversation. How was it that there were plenty of other people around me, doing things that were different but carried the same weight and never got the treatment that I did? I wondered why the Lord chose me to go through an experience where I lacked self-worth and fell into extreme depression and humiliation. Others who were making mistakes, just as I did, seemed not to experience any of these repercussions.I was so quick to compare myself to other people, but I never realized what God was trying to tell me during that time.

The Lord never intended for everyone's lives to be the same. He intended for His children to go through adversities only to strengthen us and give us a platform to share His word. God meant my time of depression, humiliation, and pain to be an obstacle to overcome. An obstacle that would lead me to see how the Lord intended to use me. He knew that my calling was to share my story to change people's lives and relate to people who go through the same feelings that I felt but to tell the story of my breakthrough with the Lord ultimately. The enemy thought that he would have the control to break me, and I will admit I gave him the power to do that for quite some time, but the Lord came and rescued me and showed me a new way of life. He transformed my heart and the way that I live every single day.

So, the Lord is saying that everyone's stories are different, and their walk with Christ, but everyone's story has a purpose. No one's story is lesser than anybody else's because nothing that the Lord created is useless. The Lord wrote your story to change someone's life, and it is important that you share your lowest of lows even when they are scared to talk about it because God has a purpose for all things that go on in your life. Don't allow the enemy to convince you of what he convinced me for a while: that I wasn't worthy enough to use my voice and my lows to change lives and show God's grace ultimately.

Your voice matters. Your story matters. It is important. Nothing that goes on in your life is insignificant. God is working on your life 24 hours of the day. The Lord is fascinated with everything that makes you who you are, and His words are written all over your story. Never forget that.

Chapter "fight" song: "See A Victory" by Elevation Worship.

"Lord, thank You for making me unique and for loving me for being different. You have a purpose for me and You took time on my plans so that I would be the best version of myself. Give me strength through the moments when I feel the least strong and remind me of who You created me to become. Help me overcome my insecurities when I compare myself to other people and allow me to trust in Your plan for my life. Thank you for taking time in my life.

Amen."

CHAPTER TEN: FORGIVE AND PRAY FOR THE PEOPLE WHO WRONG YOU

The most challenging thing for me was to forgive the people that spoke the words over me that I was less than. The words that continuously reminded me of what I had done were used as ammunition to make me feel horrible about myself. Then I realized that I was giving the people who hurt me power they did not deserve - the power to hurt me.

I also realized that spending all of my time hating them, wanting nothing good for them, was doing more damage to myself than it was to them. The hatred I had inside of me was damaging my relationship with Christ. I knew that praying for them and forgiving them was what God called me to do; however, He reminded me that did not mean that I had to associate with them, be friends with them and put myself into situations where I would hang around them. It meant that I was now able to separate myself from those toxic relationships and people and love them the way that God desired, from a distance.

God calls us to love each other. The enemy calls for us to hold things against each other. The enemy celebrates when grudges are present. For me, this meant sitting down with a handful of the people that had hurt me, made me question my worth and purpose, and letting them know face to face that I had forgiven them. Not because they asked for forgiveness, but because the Lord put that forgiveness in my heart. I told them how I pray for them and how this forgiveness is only possible because the Lord puts love and forgiveness into our hearts to rescue us from bondage.

Meeting with these people took much courage. The enemy was constantly in my head, telling me that they were not genuinely apologizing. He whispered, telling me that I was still hurt and I would always be damaged because of what they had done. This obviously caused me to question: why forgive them when they haven't reached out to me themselves? But, the Lord continued to show up. He reminded me that this was my opportunity to take the next step in my faith and show forgiveness to people whom I did not necessarily believe deserved it or had asked for it. God continued to show up in the conversation. I allowed Him to be at the center of it because I knew that I would not have been able to forgive them on my own. I needed the Lord there with me because I knew my grudge held me back from greater things. Not forgiving them caused me more harm than it did them because it separated me from the Lord.

But, in the spirit of full transparency, it took me two years to meet with these people and have those conversations. I needed to heal first to forgive them and have a mature conversation. I had to respect myself enough to wait until I was healthy and well again to have these tough conversations because if I weren't, I wouldn't have been able to handle them with grace and patient or the way that the Lord needed me to. After having these meetings, I realized that forgiving them wasn't about me at all, but instead, it was about God doing His work in our lives. I shared with them that once I let God move from the passenger seat to the driver's seat, He transformed who I was. I was able to show them that once He is given control, anything is possible. For the first time, I was able to see these girls how God saw them and was able to celebrate the fact that God continues to rescue us all. When I saw them the way Jesus did, I suddenly felt so much love in my heart for each of them. God was working! I never thought my heart could feel this way after such pain, but that's what God can do.

But, as I said before, this did not happen overnight. Forgiveness was a long process for me. During the two years I spent learning to forgive and heal, God called me to pray for them. I prayed that the Lord would show up in their lives the way He did in mine. I prayed that He would change their hearts the same way He changed mine because who was I to not wish better things for myself? The Lord's job is to protect His children, strengthen us into better versions of ourselves, and transform us into world changers.

I learned that praying for the people that hurt me frustrated the enemy. The enemy intended my grudges and hatred of these people to set me back and push me away from the positive relationship with Christ. He hoped he could hold this power over me forever. Instead of allowing that to happen, I wanted the enemy to know that I am no longer living by his rules but instead living to make Jesus known. To prove this, my actions had to show that.

I encourage you to pray for those who hurt you because we all need saving. We have all hurt people and have all had people hurt us- but we need the Lord to help us through these struggles. Listen to me very closely; you are far too worthy in the Father's eyes to living a life trying to satisfy other people and live by words that don't call you higher. So, sis, don't follow in my footsteps by drowning yourself in the thoughts and opinions of others for so long and make the change to start living by the words that the Lord has to say about you. He says you are loved, adored, and light in His Kingdom.

God calls us to glorify His name. Keeping hatred and grudges in our hearts does not glorify Him; instead, it pleases the enemy who is out to attack us. We decide to change the cycle, start doing hard things, and live like the Lord calls us to live. The thing about forgiveness is that it isn't instant. It will not happen overnight, but with time, your heart will heal, and the Lord will reveal to you just how capable He is of healing your heart to a point where instead of holding grudges against someone that hurt you, you will start living with a peace that only comes from the Lord.

Girl, the Lord's work in your life is just starting. It is nowhere near the end. Allow Him to change your heart. When you do that, I can promise you will start to live a life of peace that you never thought was possible. I believe in you, but most importantly, the Creator of this world, the One who designed every single thing about you, and the One whose name is Higher than all things believe in you. Let's live a life together that is capable of moving mountains.

Chapter "fight" song: "Holy Spirit" by Jesus Culture (feat. Kim Walker-Smith).

"Jesus, I pray for Your forgiveness over my life. To the ones that hurt me, Father, give me Your eyes, Your heart, and Your mercy. I am incapable of doing this without You. Give me the strength to put the power in Your hands and to forgive those who went behind my back and caused me pain. I pray for them. I pray that they find You and that You will become the most important thing in their life. I pray that you turn their lives into something more beautiful than they can imagine and that they will become more aware of how their actions should reflect who You are. Thank you for giving me mercy and grace.

Amen."

Reflect:

Who are some people that you need to forgive?

What do you think the steps are that you need to do to get to the point of forgiveness?

CHAPTER ELEVEN: RESPOND THE WAY JESUS WOULD

After my major challenges during the rest of my high school career, I felt like I didn't fit in. I was surrounded by people who never really took the time to know whom I turned out to be and instead focused on the mistakes that I had made. Have you ever been in a classroom or environment when you feel like the people around you are constantly judging you and waiting for you to mess up? Like you are surrounded by people who are rooting for you to make a mistake so they can reprimand you for it again instead of rooting for your success.

I have been that girl. I sat in class while other girls talked about me in their group message, saying things to bring me down. The same girls that preach on their social media accounts about following Jesus and portraying themselves as people who are out to lift girls higher, but in reality, they were saying things that brought me down to some of my lowest points, and even worse, to other girls that they even called their own friends. I have been that same girl who has had to sit there as I read from behind the shoulders of girls texting about me, not realizing that their brightness wasn't down enough for me to read what they had to say about me.

At that moment, though, I grew. I realized that I did not need to say anything to these girls. I clearly heard the Lord say, "Be my example." I froze at that moment and just prayed to the Lord. If it were me making the decision, I would have played their game and gossiped about them too, or worse, confronted them and caused a huge scene to show them that they wouldn't get away with treating people the way they were. I would have done anything to have people see their true colors. But the Lord never called me to do that.

The Lord called me to love and show the people who intentionally tried to hurt me a new side of Jesus. He called me to be an example of Him. He reminded me that I could not control who others choose to be. All I can do is lead by example with grace. I had to be true to myself and obedient to the Lord. I failed more times than I am proud of, but I knew that God was doing something far greater than I could imagine.

He wants the same for you. Instead of lashing out at people who hurt you, give the power back to the Lord. God never called you to fill the shoes of the ones who have hurt you and seek revenge. God called you to be an example of the one you follow and stand tall in confidence that the One who created you believes in your courage to walk through these hard situations with grace because you have Him by your side. I learned that by trying to live my life as a reflection of Jesus, I was able to take power away from the people who were out to get me. Instead, I gave the power to Jesus and allowed Him to deal with them on His own time. I was not responsible for their actions or choices, and therefore, it was not my responsibility to lash out at them. However, as a follower of Jesus, it was my responsibility to meet their hurtful actions with grace and prayer. I challenge you to reflect on Jesus and lean on Him when the people around you are not. You will be better because of it, and you will become an example to others.

Chapter "fight" song: "Raise A Hallelujah" by Bethel Music, Jonathan David Helser and Melissa Helser.

"Jesus, I invite you in and ask that you work through me. Take control of how I react to those who hurt me and allow me to show Your way through the way that I respond to them. Lord, I thank you for loving me and reminding me who I am during situations where others are bringing me down. I ask that you continue to remind me whom You created me to become and help guide me through trials. I love you, Jesus. Thank you for being who you are.

Amen."

Reflect:

How do you typically respond to conflict? Are you proud of the way that you respond?

What ways do you get better at how you respond to conflict and instead respond like Jesus?

CHAPTER TWELVE: REACH AND CALL OUT YOUR FEELINGS

One of the toughest things for me to overcome was allowing others the opportunity to walk alongside me through my struggles. I feared that if I let people know I was struggling and the anxiety and fear I was experiencing, it would make these feelings a reality. It was the enemy putting thoughts into my head that my feelings didn't matter. The daily internal battles made me believe that what I felt in the moment would last forever and that telling someone about it made me weak. As I have said before, during these days, I felt worthless and experienced constant anxiety. Sharing with someone my deepest thoughts about my suicidal battles was terrifying. The thoughts of acting to overcome my fears and going to someone for help was going to force me to come to terms with the reality - to accept that the world I found myself living in was not a dream.

Does that sound familiar to you? Let me give you the hope that I received and that the Lord wants you to receive at this moment. The enemy wants us to run and hide from our emotions, but the Lord wants every single part of who we are, even the parts we think make us ugly. The Lord loves you, even when you feel like you are the most unlovable person. During the days that I would bottle up all of my emotions and hide them even from those that loved me most, my family reminded me of something: talking about your darkest emotions makes you stronger. I want to give those words to you. Talking about the things that are scary and dark for you makes you stronger - not weaker. The enemy wants us to bottle everything up inside, but the Lord wants us to run straight to Him so He can fill us up with everything that will repair us.

The Lord has surrounded you with people that will help strengthen you, speak truth into you, and grow with you. And if you can't find them right now, they're coming. God sends us the people and things we need on His timeline. I learned from my experiences that walking through the tough things that you battle inside leads you to victory. Victory in Him because you are choosing to take advantage of the people and community that the Lord has generously surrounded you with. God will teach you that by doing this, you will feel less alone during the dark moments.

The Lord never leaves us alone. We often find ourselves feeling that way because the enemy tries to convince us of it. But, when you choose to view the world through the eyes of Jesus instead of your own, you will realize that you are surrounded by a father who never allows you to walk through your battles alone and graciously covers you with people whose heart aches for you and with you.

So, I challenge you to share your struggles. Instead of hiding, turn your struggles into victory by sharing them and accepting advice from the people that God has gifted you with. No more battling the things that the enemy has put into our minds and playing by the rules that the enemy wants you to follow. Instead, live along with the handbook of the One who passionately pursues you and watches out for you day in and day out. Nobody promised the road would be easy, but the Lord promises that nothing is impossible through Him.

Chapter "fight" song: "Nothing Else" by Cody Carnes.

"Jesus, I give You all of who I am - the good, the bad, and the ugly. I lift all of the things that I fear that I struggle with and have anxieties about over to You. Turn my imperfections into beauty. Make me see life through Your lenses and allow me to fill a life according to Your plan. Thank You for making me into someone you are proud of and loving me because of my struggles.

Amen."

Reflect:

What are your biggest fears?

CHAPTER THIRTEEN: YOU DESERVE TO BE HERE

It is the easiest thing in the world to allow the enemy to come into your hardest time and manipulate your mind into thinking that you're worthless. The enemy delights in making you think you have nothing to offer and that others would be better off without you. I was at that moment in my life. All the greatest things in my life, all of the things that I had worked so hard for and invested my life and time in, went crashing down. It crashed down in a single moment when I made a careless decision and acted in a wrong manner. That decision got me down to my knees, asking the Lord to take me because I was done. But, He never did.

That made me angry with God. Here I was on my bathroom floor, broken and suffering, and He continued to allow me to wake up the next morning. There were thoughts about just ending my life because I thought it would be the easiest solution. That the people that we're constantly using the video as ammunition to try to destroy me would finally get the solution, they wanted. But, the Lord gave me a vision - the vision of one of my family members finding me. The phone calls that my family would have to make to the people that helped walk me through this journey and who gave their everything to pour strength into my world when I felt like I didn't have any left of my own. The Lord so clearly said to me, "They don't win. You win by having a story that collided with Me, and it's your responsibility to share your story to save other people's lives." At that moment, the Lord reminded me that so many people feel the same emotions as me and that I'm not alone. But, when I finally decided that I would dive deeper into my relationship with the Lord and that I was ready to be healed, everything changed. The Lord gave me a bigger picture. He showed me my strength. He showed me all of the trials, accomplishments, and overcoming that I would have after those endless nights on my bathroom floor begging Him to take me. I felt the Lord tell me as I spent time reflecting, "Ray, you deserved to be here in My Kingdom even at the lowest and darkest moments," and that is exactly what the Lord wants you to know that **you** are meant to be in His Kingdom because you are needed.

You are so valuable in the transformation of His Kingdom, and He needs your beautiful soul to work with Him to change the lives of the people in desperate need of the Father. Our Gracious and loving Lord has crafted you into something magnificent, and He sees so much beauty in your brokenness. Our God is willing to invest time, sweat, and tears in you to help turn your brokenness into something that you can view yourself as worthy and beautiful that you truly are. You have to believe in yourself that with the power of the Holy Spirit invested in you, you are capable of conquering the world that is put in front of you.

No part of you is worthless or meaningless. The truth is the opposite of that - God handcrafted every single part of who you are to be a voice and change this world, even the broken part of you. Let's get off of the bathroom floor together and conquer the brokenness inside of us. Let's lift our hands high to the One that says that you deserve to be here.

Chapter "fight" song: "Rescue" by Lauren Daigle - imagine these words are being spoken directly to you from the Father.

"Father, thank You for making me on purpose. Please give me the strength that I need to get through the hardest days and the times when I feel like a mistake. Thank You for never regretting creating me and for having mercy over my life. Thank You for being active in my life. I pray that You continue to fill me up with everything from You and that you will continue to rescue me when I get off track.

Amen."

Reflect:

What thoughts are running through your mind when you feel like you are not enough and like you don't deserve to be here?

During those moments, think of ways that you can get yourself out of those situations. For me - I went sitting in my room, pulling out my phone, and listening to worship music. Another way for me to get out of that mindset was getting out of the house and spending time with my friends to get my mind off of everything.

CHAPTER FOURTEEN: YOUR TIME IS COMING - TRUST IN GOD'S TIMING

As I am writing this book, I am facing decisions in my life that are crucial. I am a week away from turning 18. The Lord has walked me down a path during the past few years that have forced me to grow up. It forced me to be stronger. To be better. And for that, I'm grateful. I'm grateful for the path because now I know that I can overcome the impossible. That doesn't mean that we won't continue to go through periods of life where we feel we have reached our dead-end. The Lord never promised us that. But, He does promise that at the end of each path, we will be better than we could have ever possibly imagined because it was His Will, not our own.

At this very moment, I am uncertain of my future. I am uncertain where I will go to college and spend the next four years of my life. I know where I want to go, but the enemy is trying to block my view of understanding where the Lord needs me to go. The same could be happening for you.

It could be the same decision as me, or whether or not that boy is good for you if you should give that boy one more chance even after he has broken your heart once or twice before. It could be whether or not you want to participate in an activity or sports team. Regardless of the scenario, the feeling of the unknown is scary because if you are anything like me, you like to be in control. You like to plan out your future and have everything figured out. But, I am learning (for the millionth time) that there is no timing more perfect than God's.

I feel the Lord continuously telling me, "You will grow throughout this period of waiting, and during that time, you have to trust in My plan because I am not failing you." I feel the Lord wants me to speak that over to you. The Lord has our future in His hands. The Lord wants both of us to know right now that He IS working, even when we don't see it clearly. He wants us to realize that we are called to rest in peace, knowing that when the timing is right according to Him, He will deliver, and it will be better than we possibly ever imagined.

I have realized that regardless of where I end up going to college, the Lord has me covered, and it will bypass all of my expectations simply because He has His hands all over it. He has people for each of us to meet along the way. We will experience seasons of waiting, but in those times, God is working. He uses the times to teach us lessons to prepare for all He has in store for us in the future. If you feel the way that I am feeling right now, which is that the Lord has forgotten about your plans, you are wrong. I often have to remind myself of this truth.

He has never forgotten about you, me, or any of His children. Instead, He is busy working. He is intentionally and perfectly stitching things together in each of our lives for our future, our decisions, and our lives to be better than we ever thought that we deserved. Together, let's rest in the hands of Our Father, who loves us and works out our lives for us.

Chapter "fight" song: "Waymaker" by Leeland (Live).

"Father, I come to you asking for patience. I ask that you give me the clarity and the peace that I need as I am facing decisions in my life that seem foggy. I trust in You, Father, and I believe in Your power. I give You my future. I give You my life. I give it all to You so that You are the only one in this world with the very best interest in my life. You are the only one that is capable of turning a horrible situation into something beautiful. Thank You for being trustworthy and for taking Yours on my life. Thank You for caring for me and loving me enough to do that for me. I trust you.

Amen."

Reflect:

Close your eyes and think of a thing(s) that you are most frustrating and hurtful in your life. Write them down. Then, try to picture God in the situation. Try to imagine the ways that God is trying to teach you through those hard moments.

CLOSING THOUGHTS: IT'S OUR TURN TO MAKE A STAND

It's time. It's time to show the people and the situations that hurt you that they no longer have power over you. It is your time to show them that their words no longer define you or have power over you. The best way to do that is to serve the Lord and only allow the things that God has to say about you and shape you. It is time to wave the haters goodbye and let them work on themselves as you move on and continue to live a life that God intended for you. To live out the plans that are paved in your path without looking back on the past and what the past brought your way. It is okay to let those things go and give the control back to the Lord. He deserves that control, and if you took anything from these chapters, I hope that it was that God has no intention of failing you, and that is something that He would never do. He is in the works of providing the best path for you and is willing to do whatever it takes to fill your life with nothing more than growth, love, and true happiness that can only be found in Him. I am proud of you, but the Lord is even more proud of you. Your journey isn't over yet, and there are more highs and lows along the way, but you always have the greatest Protector to lean upon when those lows show up. Here's to a new life of allowing God to take control and putting the past behind us.

Where am I now? I am currently closing this book during the 2020 COVID-19 pandemic. I am gratefully surrounded by family, friends, and mentors in my life who continue to pour their hearts out to me. I am stronger than I have ever been, and I am not willing to give attention to anyone trying to stab me in the back. I am months from settling down in a new state for college in hopes of pursuing a career as a mental health therapist. I am reminded daily to have the grace that the Lord has on my life, and I am working hard every day to become the person that He intended for me to become. Every day I have to remind myself of the things that I have overcome and continue to fight the battle of anxiety and depression that once took over my life. I have more fighting to go, but I refuse to give up and go back to the places I once was. Thank **you** for being a part of my journey with me and allowing me to be vulnerable with you and being vulnerable with the reflections and with your relationship with the Lord. I'm proud of you.

xox Ray

DEDICATION: TO THE ONES WHO STOOD BY MY SIDE (YOU KNOW WHO YOU ARE)

I wanted to take time within this book to thank those who stood by my side while overcoming my struggles. For seeing the good in me when other people were so eager to tear me down and make me out to be someone that I wasn't. Thank you for all of the times that you lightened up my darkness. Thank you for all of the times that you have sat there with me as I cried in your arms, for praying with me and for me, for battling with me. Thank you for loving me enough to stay for the outcome of what this tragedy took me on and for reminding me of my strength and growth process. Thank you for all of the notes, the texts checking in, and the text audios sent my way throughout all of these years. Thank you to the four best friends that showed up at my house unannounced that one night that sat in the grass with me as I was desperately trying to catch my breath from crying, holding me so tight, crying with me, and then afterward, sitting in the back of the truck with me allowing me to get my mind off of it. Thank you to the woman (and her family) who sat with me at a baseball game, talking all about the things that were going on inside of my head and offering me words of wisdom that I needed so desperately at the time. And to the woman (and her family) who sat in the grass of a T-ball practice to guide me through the bullying that I was facing even two years after the incident. Thank you to the families that stood by my family and were there for my family during the hardest time of our lives. All of the ones that came into my life after the situation and loved me for the growth that I had made. My senior year English teacher had my back and sat with me on her floor as I cried because it was too painful for me to with take myself. All of you took part in saving our family and constantly reminding us that God is in the works, and He will make this better than we ever imagined. You all are true examples of true friends that have turned into family. I love you all forever, and I could never repay you all for all of the love you all poured out to my family and me. I saw the Lord work in more ways than I possibly imagined. I was able to see the growth and strength of the people around me because of my story. I saw some girls and people at school become better people because of how God was working. I will never take that for granted.

CREDITS

Holy Bible: NIV: New International Version . Christian Media Bibles, 2016.

Cover Photographer: Madison Renee Photography

9 781649 694690